Thomas Mervyn Bouchier Marshall

The Russell Album

A Memorial of the late Reverend John Russell

Thomas Mervyn Bouchier Marshall

The Russell Album
A Memorial of the late Reverend John Russell

ISBN/EAN: 9783337345884

Printed in Europe, USA, Canada, Australia, Japan

Cover: Foto ©Raphael Reischuk / pixelio.de

More available books at **www.hansebooks.com**

THE RUSSELL ALBUM

A Memorial

OF THE LATE

REV. JOHN RUSSELL

CONTAINING

A Series of Twelve Hunting Sketches

By T. M. B. MARSHALL

With an Introduction by C. A. Mohun-Harris

DEDICATED BY PERMISSION TO H.R.H. THE PRINCE OF WALES

LONDON

BICKERS AND SON, 1 LEICESTER SQUARE

1885

The Russell D'Oyly Napkins.

HE material reminiscences of one of mark, who has passed away to his long home, to the sorrow of his family and to the regret—it might be truly said to the grief—of all with whom he was acquainted, are affectionately treasured by the surviving associates of his many pleasures in life, in response to the sentiment of the poet:

> "As looks a father on the things
> Of his dead son, I look on these."—*Maud.*

Not less have these memorials an interest to those who value the relic of a departed celebrity, in the light of an historic record that unites the present with the past, free from aught save the remembrance and the admiration of departed worth.

The dispersion of the Russell relics at the Rectory at Black Torrington brought together a large concourse of persons, both far and near, of every grade and quality, all anxious to possess themselves of a memorial of one whom in life they delighted to cherish and to honour, and, from H.R.H. the Prince of Wales to the Romany of the Wild Moor, the same anxiety prevailed to possess themselves of a treasured token, of something that had once been familiarly used by this distinguished gentleman, the recipient of many a blessing of the poor and needy to whom he was ever a generous benefactor and friend in the hour of need, and the hero of many a sporting tale. " Relics," writes that brilliant authoress, Ouida, " are like the casket of silver that held the ashes of death."

On the dispersion of these relics at Black Torrington, no article attracted more attention and caused greater competition than the famed D'Oyly Napkins. They were the clever work of the late Mr. Thomas Bourchier Marshall, a cousin of the late Mr. Mervyn Marshall. The latter kept hounds at Blagdon, and hunted a portion of the Broadbury country. Like the late Mr. Edward Duppa, the friend of Sir William Molesworth and Mr. Collier, Mr. Bourchier. Marshall adopted the profession of a painter, and was the only pupil of Mr. S. A. Hart, Professor of Painting in the Royal Academy. Mr. Russell had often admired the dessert napkins of the Mess of the North Devon Yeomanry Hussars, and, being an old friend and associate in many a long run, Mr. Marshall painted, in the D'Oyly mode, in Indian ink, a set on the subject in which both delighted. The set passed into the hands of 'Mr. Russell's old friend Mr. Linnington Ash. Such is the brief outline of the history of these D'Oyly Napkins, the origin or qualifying cause of which name has caused no little trouble to elucidate. Thus much is certain.

The origin of the name would appear to be as follows :—Some ladies belonging to a family of eminence, of the name of D'Oyly—accomplished artists—painted in Indian ink, on some dessert napkins, various clever and graceful subjects, and made them presents to their friends. They attracted much notice, and were generally admired. The process of the painting being made known, it was generally adopted, still reserving the name of the first proficients, D'Oyly. A lady residing at the time in Devonshire, and an acquaintance of the Misses D'Oyly, painted several, together with some vignettes, at the end of the first edition of " The Lay of the Last Minstrel," and a drawing of an unfinished vignette, giving a clarion scene in " Marmion," was sent to that lady by Miss D'Oyly herself. This is not conjecture, but fact, and " The Lay of the Last Minstrel " and "Marmion," with the vignettes, may be seen in a private library in this county. It was said that Miss D'Oyly had been instructed in the art by a French refugee. Certain it is that, until the beginning of the century, the name of D'Oyly had never been heard in reference to the dessert napkins.

The Russell D'Oylies are now reproduced by the aid of photography, and brought out in the shape of an Album, dedicated, by permission, to H.R.H. the Prince of Wales, the ever true and kind friend of the distinguished gentleman and sportsman.

The ancestors of Mr. Russell came into Devonshire in the year 1551—*temp*. Edw. VI. They belonged to the family of Russell of Kingston Russell, bearing the same arms, with the well-known motto, " Che sarà sarà," and accompanied their kinsman Lord Russell into the West at the time of the Roman Catholic riots at Sampford Courtenay. Mr. Russell, being a clergyman, was sent to Crediton to preach and to uphold Protestantism against the attacks of Rome, for which he suffered in the ensuing reign of Mary, but was restored to his Protestant cure at the accession of Elizabeth. Since that time the Russell family remained in the north of Devon, having allied themselves to many families of local distinction. They have been noted for ability and personal advantages. It has been stated in the Russell memoirs (Davies, p. 2) that Mr. Russell, senior, took pupils when residing in the neighbourhood of Dartmouth, and, having a pack of harriers, kept a pony-hunter, on which the boy who had made most marks during the week had a privileged mount for the next meet. Mr. Russell, senior, had a reputation for talent, both in the pulpit and in the reading desk—a distinction that descended to his late son; and he was also not less known for the aptitude of his classical quotations and conversational wit. His passages of arms with the late Sir John Rogers—both skilled combatants—at the after-dinner parties of the Chumleigh Club, which have been recorded in the racy lyrics of the late George Templer of Stover, formed one of the most lively features of that sporting meeting.

The Russell brothers, John, William, and Michael—each standing six feet—were well favoured and of goodly presence, and their only sister, Leonora (afterwards Mrs. Riccard, of South Molton), had more than an ordinary share of beauty, wit, and sparkling repartee. Many specimens of her wit and pungent satire might be recorded, but upon the Papal principle of " Pax urbi et orbi,"—not without regret,—they are withheld. Suffice to say, that of the brilliant sallies, one especially was keenly relished by the celebrated wit Jekyl, and raised a smile on the sardonic countenance of Sir Samuel Romilly, who was on a visit at the time in the neighbourhood of the accomplished lady.

Never was the apothegm—" noscitur à sociis "—more aptly illustrated than in the case of Russell, and he never belonged to that squadron of western bucolics known in the central shires by the designation of " sink the wind." His earliest friends by whom he was initiated in the science of fox-hunting were the late George Templer of Stover, the Rev. Harry Templer, most accomplished gentlemen, and the Hon. Newton Fellowes. These may be said to have been his sporting godfathers, and in after-years his social allies were J. Bulteel, Charles Trelawny, Sir Walter Carew, Sir John Duntze, Rev. Harry Farr Yeatman, Sir Arthur Chichester, Sir Henry B. Wrey, W. Coryton, Paul Treby, Arthur Mohun-Harris, styled in the Davies Memoirs " the Coadjutor," F. Glanville, T. J. Phillipps, Admiral Parker, W. Harris, Moore Stevens, R. Sleeman, J. Morth Woolcombe, Sir W. Raleigh Gilbert, Rev. Pomeroy Gilbert, J. Clode Braddon, George Williams (Scorrier House), Walter Radclyffe, Burlton Bennett, Pryce Mitchell, F. Scobell, H. and J. Deacon, J. Whidborne, Gage Hodge, A. Lock, Froude Bellew, L. Bencraft, and J. L. Davies, and, later in life, the Duke of Beaufort, Earl of Portsmouth, Lord Poltimore, Sir W. Molesworth, Whyte Melville, Anstruther Thompson, and Henry Villebois. He never varied in temper nor in character, and to one and all he was ever the same simple, kind-hearted, and brilliant associate. "His readiness and ability to help ladies in the stag-hunting field have been already alluded to, and from the eulogistic terms in which he never failed to speak of a few as 'elegant and accomplished horse-women' who, whatever the pace, were wont to take a brilliant lead, and look to no one for help, so long as their horses could gallop, and they could help themselves." First and foremost come Miss Kinglake, now the Hon. Mrs. T. Fitz-William, "one of the best," as Russell writes, "I ever saw from find to finish on Exmoor," her sister Miss Beata Kinglake, Lady Lovelace, Mrs. Henry Deane, Mrs. Pulsford Browne, a very fine rider, who went as straight over a country as a bird on the wing. Then there were Miss Clara Jekyll, Mrs. Wynch, Mrs. John Luttrell, Miss Leslie, the three Miss Taylors of Dulverton, Miss Julia Carwithen, now Mrs. Pyne Coffin, Miss Luttrell, Miss Whidborne, Mrs. Louis and Mrs. Russell Riccard, Mrs. James Turner, Miss Vibart, Lady Lindsay, Mrs. Procter Baker, Miss Constance Baxendale, and Mrs. Lock Roe. Then, last in the list, but rarely so in the chase, come Mrs. Granville Somerset, and her sister, Mrs. Cholmondeley, two ladies whom Russell described as worthy of niches in the grandest temple ever dedicated to the Forest Queen."—(Davies, p. 351.) To this Russell list might have been added the Misses Carew of Marley, the Misses Parker and Stuart Hawkins, ever in the front rank with the Dartmoor hounds.

Russell never recovered the change from his own happy Tordown, at Swymbridge, to the more lucrative Rectory at Black Torrington. He had, however, a pack of fox-hound harriers that were simply perfection, and on his last birthday, being incapable of field exertion, and upon the advice of his medical friend and physician, Mr. Linnington Ash, the hounds took their departure for the kennel of Mr. Baring, at Membland, near Plymouth. His old friend and ally Mohun-Harris came to visit him on that day, and, in lamenting the departure of his favourites, the tears trickled down his cheeks, especially in speaking of one "Henbane," whom he said "could see scent," and who had been reserved with another couple, and, had life been spared him with an accession of health, they would, without doubt, have formed the nucleus of another pack. He was much affected at seeing his old friend and ally of over half a century on this which was his last birthday, but after dinner with Mr. Linnington Ash, he recovered his spirits, and talked over the runs over Broadbury, with accompanying anecdotes, in his wonted and cheery way. "Mind, Arthur," were his last words, "that you give an especial account in *Baily* of my dear, dear hounds, and remember 'Henbane.'" He expatiated with affectionate gratitude on the many acts of kindness that he had received at Sandringham from their Royal Highnesses the Prince and Princess of Wales, and of the latter he ever delighted to speak in terms of unbounded admiration. Mr. Henry Villebois came from Norfolk, at the desire of H.R.H., in the hope of being able to convey favourable intelligence. Russell subsequently went to Bude for change of air, without any good effects, and, returning home, passed away rapidly, but without pain, and in peace and love with all, "in spe beatæ resurrectionis."

M. H.

GOING TO COVER. - THE OLD COUNTRY SQUIRE.

"Like a fine old English Gentleman,   "A matchless steed, though something old,
 "One of the olden time."   "Prompt in his paces, cool and bold."

NEC REGE NEC POPULO, SED UTROQUE

Manet sub Jove frigido   No. 2.   Venator teneræ conjugis immemor

BREAKING COVER. — The Aristocracy.

"Abiit, excessit, evasit, erupit."

Cicero in Catilinam.

!

THE ARMY.

"He was a man of martial mould;
"Proud was his front, his bearing bold,
"His seat in saddle fair."

THE FLOWERS OF THE FIELD.

"Over the Water."

"He staid not for brake, and
he stopped not for stone;
"He swam the Eske river where
ford there was none."

"For once, upon a raw and gusty day,
"The troubled Tyber chafing with her shores,
"Cæsar said to me,—Darest thou, Cassius, now
"Leap in with me into this angry flood,
"And swim to yonder point?"—

"The effort was in vain.
"The spur-stroke failed to rouse the horse;
"Wounded & weary, in mid course
"He stumbled on the plain."

"Woe worth the chace! woe worth
the day!
"That cost thy life, my gallant
grey!"

THE DEATH. "Last scene of all."

"Immolat et pœnam scelerato ex sanguine sumit
"Fervidus: ast illi solvuntur frigore membra,
"Vitaque cum gemitu fugit indignata sub umbras."
Æn. XII. 949. 951. 952.

"The chieftains then
"Blew the recall, & from their perfect work
"Returned rejoicing." Southey.

ΤΕΛΟΣ